RAVEN'S LIGHT

RAVEN'S LIGHT

A Myth from the People of the Northwest Coast

Retold by Susan Hand Shetterly
Illustrated by Robert Shetterly

ATHENEUM 1991 NEW YORK
COLLIER MACMILLAN CANADA
Toronto
MAXWELL MACMILLAN INTERNATIONAL PUBLISHING GROUP
New York Oxford Singapore Sydney

This book is dedicated to Chac,
the wild raven we raised and released,
and to Sadie, his friend

Text copyright © 1991 by Susan Hand Shetterly
Illustrations copyright © 1991 by Robert Shetterly

Atheneum
Macmillan Publishing Company
866 Third Avenue
New York, NY 10022

Collier Macmillan Canada, Inc.
1200 Eglinton Avenue East
Suite 200
Don Mills, Ontario M3C 3N1

First edition
Printed in Hong Kong
1 2 3 4 5 6 7 8 9 10

Library of Congress Cataloging-in-Publication Data

Shetterly, Susan Hand, 1942-
Raven's Light: A Myth from the People of the Northwest Coast/retold
by Susan Hand Shetterly; illustrated by Robert Shetterly.—1st ed.
p.   cm.
Summary: Explains how Raven made the earth, animals, moon, and
sun.
ISBN 0-689-31629-1
1. Indians of North America—Northwest, Pacific—Legends.
[1. Indians of North America—Northwest, Pacific—Legends.]
I. Shetterly, Robert, ill.   II. Title.
E78.N77S54   1991
398.2'089970795—dc20
[E]   89-78183   CIP   AC

RAVEN'S LIGHT

Raven winged through the dark carrying a small, round stone. A heavy sack hung around his neck.

Above the churning waves he flew with the stone and the sack until he grew so tired he could hardly lift his wings.

One more flap, he thought.

Then, slowly, one more.

His eyes began to close. His head began to droop.

Suddenly, the stone slipped from his beak and fell. It plunked into the water.

"Carragh!" he cried. He beat his wings against the waves until the waves around him calmed. In the center of that still place floated Raven's stone. But he could not pull it out.

So he held on. He rested his weight against the stone, turned his beak into the feathers of his shoulder, and fell asleep.

As Raven slept on the vast, dark sea, the stone began to grow. It stretched up into mountains and fell into valleys. It flattened out into plateaus that spread away under the stars. Raven woke and saw that he was standing on a high crag. He looked around. Nothing moved. The mountains and valleys and bare plateaus seemed to be waiting for something.

Raven reached into the sack and pulled out a lodgepole
pine. He dropped it and tilted his head to listen to it fall. He
heard it creak as it stood up, and whoosh as it straightened
out its branches.

One by one, he threw out a mountain goat, a grizzly bear,
an aspen tree, a marmot, a pika, a gray wolf, a longhorn
beetle, and a peregrine falcon. He looked through his sack
and grabbed a spadefoot toad and dropped it down, too.

He heard the grizzly stand up and shake herself. He
heard the feet of the wolf tick across the rocks. He heard
the wings of the falcon snap open and beat away into
the dark.

Raven chuckled to himself.

He took off the sack. He stretched his neck and shook his
wings. In the pale light from the distant stars, he preened
each feather until he glistened like a dark star himself.

Then Raven sang a song. His voice rattled over the new
land.

"Arrak! Arrak!" he sang. "Gak! Gak! Arrak!"

When he had finished, Raven put on the sack again. He leaned down and picked up a small, round stone. With a little jump, he leaped into the air and skimmed over the water until, once more, he grew so tired that the stone slipped from his beak.

And that is how Raven made the earth. He pulled out of his sack the snakes, and the sleek fishes, the people, the moose, the mule deer, the horseshoe crabs, the winter wrens, the blue-eyed grasses, the snowshoe hare, and every other animal and plant. Gently, he dropped them all. He listened to them fall.

Raven knew that the earth was beautiful. He flew above the forest and saw the gleam of the wolf's eyes through the trees. He flapped to the bank of a river and saw the sharp glint of the bear's teeth. He watched the salmon fight their way upstream, a froth of silver bubbles breaking from their sides. And he stared a long time at the people as they moved back and forth through the dark.

But he could see them only by the light of the distant stars.

A rip at the top of the sky snapped in the wind. Raven flew close and put his eye up to it and peered in. There he saw the Kingdom of the Day, and a chief sitting at the entrance to his house, wrapped in a blaze of light.

Raven flew down and looked once more at his dark world. "Rawk!" he screamed.

He jumped into the air. When he found the rip again, he ruddered his tail and swerved into absolute brightness.

He crossed a stream. A young woman was kneeling beside it, dipping her bowl in the water.

Raven spun around. Changing himself into a piece of cedar frond, he fell and floated on the stream. He drifted into her bowl and she drank him down.

Her name was White Feather. She was the daughter of the Great Chief.

Before the year was done, the Great Chief invited all the people of his kingdom to a potlatch, a feast to celebrate the birth of White Feather's first child. The guests wore their finest wooden masks, their eagle feathers, and their grass skirts. They beat drums. They danced around the tall totems. In quavery voices, they sang ancient songs to the newborn boy.

The old shaman, older than the stones in the stream, danced alone. Like a dry leaf pushed by a gust of wind, he skittered over the ground, up to the child, and with a bony hand lifted the blanket from the boy's shoulder.

"Wings!" he howled.

The drums rolled to a stop. The dancers froze. Slowly, the Great Chief rose from his throne of caribou hides. Through the silence of the people, he approached White Feather.

"Let me see this grandson of mine," he said. She drew off the blanket. The baby lay asleep. On each shoulder sprouted the merest tuft of black feathers.

The Great Chief touched them with his fingers.

"Those are not wings, Father," whispered White Feather. "But a hero's mark. A sign that your grandson will be like you."

"I have no feathers," her father growled.

"A trick! A trick!" shrieked the shaman, spinning in a circle beneath the totem.

"This boy will do good, Father," said White Feather. A tear fell from her cheek and splashed against her son's belly. The child stirred.

"I do not want to see those feathers again," her father said. He sighed, turned away, and walked heavily to his throne.

The drums began again. The guests resumed the dance. The shaman climbed to the top of the totem, crossed his arms and legs, and became as still as the wood itself.

The little boy grew. He was a clever and good child. White Feather dressed him in a cape woven from the soft inner bark of the cedar tree. And soon his grandfather forgot about the black feathers hidden beneath the cape.

The Great Chief spent hours teaching the little boy how to carve small figures and how to follow the tracks of animals. He kept the Day in a round basket that hung from the center pole of his house.

Sometimes the little boy reached out his hands toward the basket and cried, "Arrak! Arrak!"

"What does he mean by that?" his grandfather asked.

"He wants to play with the Day," said White Feather. She smiled at the boy.

"No one touches it," the Great Chief warned.

But one day the little boy reached toward the basket and his cries grew louder. Even White Feather could not comfort him.

The Great Chief groaned. "I cannot sleep!" he protested. "Give the boy the Day if you must!"

So White Feather untied the basket and handed it to the boy, who played with it quietly as his grandfather rested. When he awoke, the boy handed the basket back to him, and the grandfather gathered the child up into his lap.

"Years ago," he began, "when this kingdom was very small, we lived in darkness. But in a world above our own, I saw a light rise and set. Over and over. Well, my little one, I took it and set it in that basket that you like so much. Now my kingdom knows no dark."

The boy listened quietly to his grandfather's words, but before long, he cried out for the Day again.

"Oh, give it to him!" said the Great Chief. "Who can abide such racket?"

And soon the boy was allowed to play with the Day whenever he wanted.

Once White Feather left the boy and went gathering kindling in the forest, and the Great Chief left the boy to follow the tracks of a deer over the hillside.

When the sleeping shaman opened an eye, he saw the boy carry the basket of the Day outside. He saw him walk to the place where the sky was torn, holding the basket.

"Thief! Thief!" screamed the shaman.

The boy dived through the hole. As he fell, his cape floated away. His black wings spread. His feet turned to claws, his mouth to a beak.

Behind him, the Kingdom of the Day swirled into darkness and disappeared.

Animals looked up as Raven passed overhead, coasting above a broad river that emptied into the sea. In the shallows moved men and women and children netting salmon.

"Throw me a fish, and I'll drop you the Day!" Raven called.

"We don't need the Day," they grumbled. "And we can't waste a fish."

"But I have brought it here for you!" Raven insisted.

"Go away, Raven," they answered. "We see well enough as it is."

"Raugh!" yelled Raven in a rage. "You don't even know the colors of the fish you catch, you stubborn people! I will drop the Day into the sea and it will be lost forever!"

But a small girl held up her hands. She had seen the shafts of light streaming from Raven's beak.

"Wait!" she called. She reached into the river, grabbed a fish, and flung it into the sky.

Raven caught it. He let go of the basket, which fell to

Sitting on the bank with the basket in her lap, the girl pulled loose a strand. A wide burst of light rose into the air like a golden river. It spun softly, round and round, up into the sky and hung there. It was the moon.

Raven chuckled to himself from the top of a pine.

The girl drew away more basket strands. Sunlight streamed from the unraveling. Her people left the riverbed and gathered around her as light bathed the eastern hill. They turned to follow it with their eyes.

"Ah!" the people cried when they saw that the aspen leaves were yellow.

"Oh!" they sighed as the needles on the pine trees turned a deep, rich green.

"Ha! Ha! Ha!" Raven laughed from the treetop.